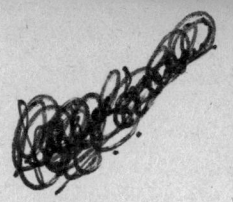

HOW THE SMART COOKIE CRUMBLES . . .

1. What's the difference between a five-cent soft drink can and a thirty thousand dollar car?

2. What is the scientific proof that insanity is hereditary?

3. What is the penalty for bigamy?

4. Why should you never criticize your wife?

5. Why should you never lend money to friends?

Answers:
1. Toss the can along the highway and it will last forever, but no matter how well you care for the car, it will rust out in three years. 2. You can get it from your children. 3. Two mothers-in-law. 4. If she were perfect, she'd have married better. 5. It ruins their memory.

WISE CRACKERS FOR SMART COOKIES

This is JOE

An agglomeration of Better Mottoes and Wise Cracks collected by official parade horse Joe, chairman of the Let's Have Better Mottoes Association, Inc.

—with an introduction by John Yeck

FAWCETT CREST • NEW YORK

Sale of this book without a front cover may be unauthorized. If this book is coverless, it may have been reported to the publisher as "unsold or destroyed" and neither the author nor the publisher may have received payment for it.

A Fawcett Gold Medal Book
Published by Ballantine Books
Copyright © 1992 by John D. Yeck

All rights reserved under International and Pan-American Copyright Conventions. Published in the United States by Ballantine Books, a division of Random House, Inc., New York, and simultaneously in Canada by Random House of Canada Limited, Toronto.

Library of Congress Catalog Card Number: 92-90162

ISBN 0-449-14747-9

Manufactured in the United States of America

First Edition: September 1992

Introduction

This book consists of happy thoughts garnered from wastebaskets, walls, freeway overpasses, bumper stickers, fortune cookies, boxcars, the next table at lunch, library books, and the like, by members of the Let's Have Better Mottoes Association, Inc. and forwarded to its chairman and official parade horse, JOE, for the Association's collection. Portions of that collection are contained in this book.

The Let's Have Better Mottoes Association, Inc. is a loose confederation of thoughtful, scholarly, like-minded individuals who have been overly bombarded by inspirational, moralistic, motivational, stimulating mottoes or "golden thoughts" such as:

**People who live in glass houses
shouldn't throw stones.**

They've concluded that such thoughts are an affront to human nature, obviously outdated, and should very probably be outlawed by Congress.

Instead, they search for and circulate *better* mottoes, which strike much closer to eternal truths, such as:

**People who live in stone houses
shouldn't throw glasses**

or, perhaps:

**People who live in glass houses
shouldn't get stoned.**

These have been arranged in the book so they can be easily clipped out and posted or distributed where they will do the most good.

In addition to mottoes, members have also searched for other short expressions of wisdom, or Wise Crackers, which clearly reflect life's little realities, such as:

The first thing a kid learns after he gets a drum for Christmas is that he won't get another one.

In spite of his scholarly appearance and carefully cultivated aura of brilliance, JOE makes no claim to the origination of all Mottoes and Wise Crackers.

They are excerpts from a decades-long collection that has gradually increased as the winds of chance blew them into JOE's stall or across his path, where he intercepted, expanded, abbreviated, or merely recorded those that caught his fancy, without regard whence they came.

We recommend that you approach the collection gingerly, savor each item slowly, digesting only a few at a sitting. Then identify your favorites, adopt them, and amaze your friends and co-workers with your sparkling wit.

Used carefully and selectively over a period of several months, JOE's gems will build your reputation as an amusing, droll, entertaining, clever, witty, fairly funny person. No extra charge. Accept your new status gracefully . . . and stay humble. And if you happen to run into *better* mottoes not included, just send them to P.O. Box 225, Dayton, OH 45401-0225 and they'll be promptly forwarded to JOE.

JOHN YECK
Member, LHBMA, I.

WISE CRACKERS FOR SMART COOKIES

IT ISN'T WHETHER YOU WIN OR LOSE
BUT HOW YOU PLACE THE BLAME

Chuckle du jour:

An unemployed jester is nobody's fool.

Association News:

Our Committee on Daffynitions submits for approval: Floods are when Rivers get too big for their Bridges; a Hangover is the Bad Time you get absolutely free with a Good Time; and a Reckless Driver is one who passes you no matter how much you speed up.

Chuckle du jour:

Politics is a promising career.

Association News:

The Association's ad hoc Stop-and-Think-about-It Committee points out that: While it's no fun playing against a poor loser, it's better than playing against any kind of winner; in the olden days they called people "liberal" when they were generous with their own money; and Middle Age is right on—more age and more middle.

IF AT FIRST YOU DON'T SUCCEED
SO MUCH FOR SKYDIVING

HE WHO HESITATES GETS BUMPED FROM THE REAR

Chuckle du jour:

Some people who hanker for retirement can't even figure out what to do with a Sunday afternoon.

Association News:

The Association's Committee on Daffynitions reports: Tolerance is the belief that those who disagree with you have a perfect right to be wrong; a Bargain is anything that is only moderately overpriced; and Censors are people who know more than they think you ought to.

Chuckle du jour:

Show me a good loser and I'll show you a salesman playing golf with his best customer.

Association News:

The Association's Dictionary Revision Committee reports that: "Virus" is doctor talk for "Your guess is as good as mine"; a Pessimist is an Optimist on his way home from the races; and Denial is a river in Egypt.

EARLY TO BED, EARLY TO RISE
MAKES A MAN MIGHTY TIRED BY AFTERNOON

CRIME WOULDN'T PAY IF THE GOVERNMENT RAN IT

Chuckle du jour:

Man's best friend is the hot dog. It feeds the hand that bites it.

Association News:

The Association's ad hoc Committee on Advice-Is-What-You-Give-Others-Interference-Is-What-You-Get-From-Them has come down on the side of Giving and consequently advises: The difference between playing the stock market and playing the horses is that one horse always wins; Experience is learning a lot of things you shouldn't do again; and the Ten Commandments are not supposed to be multiple choice.

Chuckle du jour:

For speedy transfer of funds, electronic banking can't touch an old-fashioned wedding.

Association News:

The Association's Committee on Rules and Regulations reports that: Variables won't, Constants aren't; summer days are longer than winter because heat expands and cold contracts; and bare feet magnetize sharp objects so they always point upward from the floor.

IT'S BETTER TO HAVE LOVED AND LOST
THAN TO DO HOMEWORK FOR ALL THOSE KIDS

PEOPLE WHO LIVE IN STONE HOUSES SHOULDN'T THROW GLASSES

Chuckle du jour:

Enjoy your kids while they're young and still on your side.

Association News:

The Association's Task Force on Strictly Show Biz reports that: The poorest magicians make audiences disappear fastest; at any flea circus a single dog in the audience can spoil the whole show; and it's getting harder and harder to support the government in the style to which it's become accustomed.

Chuckle du jour:

If ignorance is no excuse, what good is it?

Association News:

The Association's official philosopher officially opines that: A bald head is better than none at all; it pays to be truthful since you may make a hole in one while playing alone someday; and TV has changed the American child from an irresistible force to an immovable object.

MONEY ISN'T EVERYTHING
BUT IT KEEPS YOU IN TOUCH WITH THE KIDS

I LIKE POLITICAL JOKES
EXCEPT WHEN THEY GET ELECTED

Chuckle du jour:

Misery may love company, but Hilarity throws better parties.

Association News:

The Association's Health and Longevity Committee recommendations include: To keep your teeth in shape, brush twice a day, visit your dentist twice a year, and keep your nose out of other people's business; to grow old gracefully, never go mountain climbing with a beneficiary and assiduously avoid Alcoholic Rheumatism, i.e., getting stiff in joints.

Chuckle du jour:

Only undertakers and copier repairmen have true job security.

Association News:

The Association's standing Committee on Better Definitions now maintains that a Crepe Suzette is really just a flash in a pan; that Ticker Tape is that paper the doc peers at when you get an EKG; and that Conscience is the still, small voice that tells you the IRS is likely to check your return.

SILENCE IS GOLDEN SO SHUT UP AND LISTEN

❖

HE WHO HESITATES IS LAST

❖

Chuckle du jour:

You're only young once, but you can be childish all your life.

Association News:

The Association's Committee on Knowledge reports that: Lifting a cat by the tail gives one experience he can get no other way; Patience is often simply a case of not knowing what to do; and Humility is tricky: when you finally decide you've got it, you've lost it.

Chuckle du jour:

Today's generation thinks the English Channel is something on a French TV set.

Association News:

The Association's Committee on Odd Observations notes that: Old Age is when you read the obituaries before the sports page and look at the menu before you look at the waitress; consultants know exactly what to do—until it happens to them; and the chief causes of new problems are the solutions to old problems.

WATCH OUT FOR SCHOOL CHILDREN
ESPECIALLY WHEN THEY'RE DRIVING

❖

YOU SHOULD GO FAR— AND I HOPE SOON

❖

Chuckle du jour:

A shortcut is the quickest way to a place you weren't going to.

Association News:

The Association's Committee on Dictionary Updates has determined that: a Sherbet is a horse that can't lose; a Midget is the center engine of a very fast airplane; Hari-Kari is just another way of saying "have wig, will travel"; and Geometry is what an acorn says when it grows up.

Chuckle du jour:

Some who go 4th with a 5th on the 4th don't get to go 4th on the 5th.

Association News:

The Association's Committee on Dictionary Definition Revisions reports: A Boat is what you fill a hole in the water with; a Racehorse is an animal that takes thousands of people for a ride all at once; and Childhood is when the kids are both deductible and taxing.

WINNING ISN'T EVERYTHING
BUT IT SURE BEATS COMING IN SECOND

IF IT WEREN'T FOR THE LAST MINUTE NOTHING WOULD EVER GET DONE

Chuckle du jour:

Premature gray hair is hereditary—you get it from your kids.

Association News:

Whyizit, wonders Joe, that children, like canoes, perform best when paddled in the rear? That a Fat Chance and a Slim Chance mean the same? And that the world has so many Wise Crackers and so few Smart Cookies?

Chuckle du jour:

Dieting is the only game that you win by losing.

Association News:

The Undercover Committee reports that only the middle-aged pick up pennies anymore: the old can't see them and the young know they aren't worth the time; only adults can't open childproof bottles; and only scissor grinders are happy when things are dull.

ONE GOOD THING ABOUT A BAD REPUTATION:
IT'S EASY TO MAINTAIN

PEOPLE WILL BELIEVE ANYTHING
IF YOU WHISPER IT

Chuckle du jour:

The difference between cook and chef is who cleans up the kitchen.

Association News:

The Association's Committee on Simplicity in Life reports that Dieting is simple: Eat all you want of what you don't like, nothing except what you can easily afford, and if it tastes real good, spit it out; and the easy, simple way to catch a plane is to miss the one before.

Chuckle du jour:

The nice thing about smoking three packs a day is that you don't have to worry so much about eating mushrooms.

Association News:

Just remember: Those who tell you, "You can't take it with you" are fixin' to take it with them; you can't get anything clean without getting something dirty, but you can get everything dirty without getting anything clean; and most young bucks want a girl just like the girl who turned down dear old Dad.

I'M A MAN OF FEW WORDS
AS I'VE TOLD YOU A MILLION TIMES

❖

THE EARLY WORM IS FOR THE BIRDS

❖

Chuckle du jour:

A sound-good reason is sometimes better than a good, sound reason.

Association News:

The Association's Committee on Better Definitions feels that Conscience is the still, small voice that tells you *this* is the time you're going to get caught; Middle Age is when the telephone rings on Saturday night and you hope it's the wrong number; and an Optimist is a person who does crossword puzzles in ink.

Chuckle du jour:

Just when you learn to make ends meet, somebody moves the ends.

Association News:

The Association's Wisdom of the Ages Committee reports that: the best measure of success is not your home, car, or clothes, but how your kids describe you to their friends; history not only repeats itself but that's also what's wrong with it; and no matter how you figure it, gray hair probably isn't premature.

NEVER, NEVER, NEVER, *NEVER* BE REDUNDANT

❖

WHEN IN DOUBT—DELEGATE

❖

Chuckle du jour:

No one ever listens to anybody else, and if you try it for a while you'll know why.

Association News:

The Association's permanent Committee on Adolescence announces that the reason teenagers don't have hang-ups is that everything they own is on the floor; Mother's Day is when you borrow from Father to buy Mother your favorite candy; and there's nothing about teenage behavior that a bit of simple, logical reasoning won't aggravate.

Chuckle du jour:

Women like quiet men because they think they're listening.

Association News:

The Association has opened a new research lab to investigate nature: human and regular. Its first curator proved that even though hippopotamuses have no stingers in their tails, it is preferable to be sat on by a bee. The second determined that nothing spoils children worse than belonging to a neighbor. The third requests that we all stop complaining about the weather before the government decides to run it.

BEWARE OF THOSE WHO SAY THEY'RE ON YOUR SIDE . . .
SO'S APPENDICITIS

DON'T BRAG ABOUT YOUR DEGREES
I HAVE 98.6 MYSELF

Chuckle du jour:

For financial success a good education is the next-best thing to a pushy mother.

Association News:

The Association's Committee on Economic Theory and Practice reports that: Experience is a dandy teacher, but it sends huge bills; a dollar won't do as much for people as it used to, and vice versa; and while college for your kids may be expensive, it's worth it—when they're that age, you don't want to know what they're up to.

Chuckle du jour:

Listen to your conscience even though you've been told never to take advice from a stranger.

Association News:

The Association's W Committee wonders: Whyizit that Common is least Common of all the Senses? Whyizit that a cheap soft drink can, when tossed along the highway, will last forever, but a thirty thousand dollar car, given the best of care, rusts out in three years? And whyizit that people lose their health getting wealth so they can lose their wealth getting health?

ANYONE WHO THINKS TALK IS CHEAP
HASN'T TALKED TO A LAWYER

❖

MAJOR SURGERY IS WHAT *I* HAD *MINOR* SURGERY IS WHAT *YOU* HAD

❖

Chuckle du jour:

If you want to know how old you are, just watch your grandson play soccer.

Association News:

The Association's Committee on Environmental, Natural, and Unnatural Questions and Answers (ENUQA) wonders: Do Ghosts fly every witch way; are they called Lightning Bugs because they never blink in the same place twice; and do Yaks really talk a lot?

Chuckle du jour:

In the Good Old Days M stood for Mother instead of McDonald's.

Association News:

Our Commission on *Best* has determined that: The best way to keep children's clothes clean is to keep them off children; the best advice to a dieter is "No thyself"; and the best way to remember your wife's birthday is to forget it once.

DON'T RIDICULE YOUR EMPLOYEES
IF THEY WERE PERFECT, YOU'D BE WORKING FOR THEM

A FOOL AND HIS MONEY
ARE SOON ELECTED

Chuckle du jour:

What this country needs is more free speech worth listening to.

Association News:

The ad hoc Committee in Charge of the New LHBMA,I. Dictionary says: A Bath Mat is a little, dry rug that dripping children stand alongside of; a Housing Development is a place where they cut down all the trees and name the streets after them; and Experience is something you don't get until after you need it most.

Chuckle du jour:

It's called "take-home" pay because you can't afford to go anywhere else with it.

Association News:

Reports from the Committee on Comparisons reveal that: Land Developers are those who want to build cabins in the woods this year, while Conservationists are those who built theirs last year; and the difference between death and taxes is that death never gets any worse.

❖

ALL WORK AND NO PAY
MAKES A HOUSEWIFE

❖

A FRIEND IN NEED IS A FRIEND TO AVOID

Chuckle du jour:

One nice thing about having multiple personalities—you never get lonesome.

Association News:

The LHBMA,I. Committee on the High Cost of Living notes that sticker shock used to be limited to autos, but now you can get it from a pair of sneakers; that two can live as cheaply as one if one doesn't eat; and that no matter how high doctor bills get, they have postmortem charges beat by a mile.

Chuckle du jour:

A bachelor has to wash his own dishes, make his own bed, put out his own garbage, and then, a month or so later, do it all over again.

Association News:

Our Association's ad hoc Committee on Observations observes that as people grow older, their broad minds and narrow waists change places; that Truth is a science, but Lying is an art, since you're stuck with the truth but can be beautifully creative otherwise; and that a Trouble-Free Product means that the trouble you get with it carries no extra charge.

❖

GIVE ME THE FACTS STRAIGHT . . .
I CAN MIX THEM UP WHEN I QUOTE YOU

❖

❖

INSANITY IS HEREDITARY
YOU CAN GET IT FROM YOUR CHILDREN

❖

Chuckle du jour:

Success is hiring someone to mow the lawn so you can play golf for exercise.

Association News:

The Association's Committee in Charge of Problem Identification reports that: The trouble with inferiority complexes is that those who need them most don't have them; the trouble with parents is that when we get them, they're too old to change their habits; the trouble with waiting for the perfect woman is that she wants the perfect man, and vice versa.

Chuckle du jour:

Conceit works backward: it makes everybody sick but the one who has it.

Association News:

The Association's Committee on Productivity reports successful experiments in effective action, to wit: To get your kids to look up to you, turn off the TV; to stop gossiping in the office, turn the clock to 5:01; to diet effectively, take a job selling on commission.

❖

IT MATTERS NOT WHETHER YOU WIN OR LOSE

... UNTIL YOU LOSE

❖

❖

YOU ARE ONLY AS OLD AS YOU FEEL
BUT NOT NEARLY AS IMPORTANT

❖

Chuckle du jour:

If everyone obeyed the Ten Commandments, we'd have no six o'clock news.

Association News:

The Association's Whyizit Committee is at it again with its questions, to wit: Whyizit at bargain sales people fight over stuff that's been reduced because nobody wanted it in the first place? Whyizit the windshield wiper on the driver's side always streaks and wears out first? And whyizit just as you manage to make ends meet, something breaks in the middle?

Chuckle du jour:

What does an ophthalmologist call himself after his third martini?

Association News:

The Association's permanent Committee on Vice Versa, Etc., reports that: A rabbit's foot may seem lucky for some, but it certainly wasn't lucky for the rabbit; rents have finally gotten to the point where leases are breaking tenants; and good legs are what if you ain't got you can't get to first base and neither can your sister.

❖

WHEN CHOOSING BETWEEN TWO EVILS PICK THE ONE YOU'VE NEVER TRIED BEFORE

❖

❖

MISERS ARE NO FUN TO LIVE WITH
BUT AS ANCESTORS THEY'RE GREAT!

❖

Chuckle du jour:

Propaganda is what you do to straighten up a slumping male goose.

Association News:

The Association's Committee on the Price of Progress has determined that: If the safety pin had been invented now instead of years ago, it would have nine moving parts, sixteen transistors, and an annual service contract; any electronic gadget you can understand is already obsolete; and after listening to the music in a teenage department, it's hard to remember that a pretty girl is like a melody.

Chuckle du jour:

If the prime rate is what banks charge friends, who needs enemies?

Association News:

The Association's Select Committee on Business Practices points out that: Experts don't know any more than other people—they just organize it in an outline and use slides; Born Executives are those who have fathers who own the business; and with the microfiche and the silicon chip more and more entrepreneurs are ordering fiche and chips.

❖

IF YOU CAN'T SAY SOMETHING GOOD ABOUT ANYBODY, LET'S HEAR IT NOW

❖

❖

I AM *NEVER* ARBITRARY
AND I REFUSE TO DISCUSS IT FURTHER

❖

Chuckle du jour:

A vacation is when you get tired on your own time.

Association News:

The Association's Committee on Clarifying Definitions has decided that: An Individualist is different from you, an Oddball is different from me; Bigamy is simply two rites that make a wrong; and Experience is what lets you recognize a mistake the instant you've made it again.

Chuckle du jour:

Smoking is now also becoming the leading cause of statistics.

Association News:

The Association's Committee on Progress reports that: Research shows the latest computer can make as many mistakes in two seconds as it used to take twenty book-keepers twenty years to make; after you've become too old to set a bad example, you can start giving good advice; and an Old-Timer is one who can remember when paying on time meant being punctual.

❖

I NEVER FORGET A FAVOR
ESPECIALLY WHEN I DO IT

❖

IT ISN'T WHETHER YOU WIN OR LOSE
IT'S HOW MUCH

Chuckle du jour:

Being beyond medical help may only mean you have a cold in the head.

Association News:

The Association's Might-Have-Been Committee reports that: Intelligence tests only prove how smart you would have been not to take them; rock groups can afford those electronic gizmos because of what they save on music lessons; and the quickest way to find a missing right glove is to throw away the left.

Chuckle du jour:

Frequent naps will keep you from getting old—especially if taken while you're driving on a freeway.

Association News:

The Association's Whyizit Committee has been active again and has asked the membership assembled: Whyizit people park their cars in driveways and drive their cars on parkways? Whyizit that the time traffic hardly moves at all is called rush hour? And whyizit people with "a great deal for you" say they want to let you in when what they want to do is take you in?

❖

YOU'RE ONLY YOUNG ONCE
BUT YOU CAN BE IMMATURE FOREVER

❖

TODAY'S THE TOMORROW YOU DREADED YESTERDAY

... AND NOW YOU KNOW WHY

Chuckle du jour:

Work is what you get when you don't want it, don't like when you get it, and do only so that some day you won't have to.

Association News:

The Association's Can't-Win Committee reports that: By the time your son is old enough not to be ashamed of you, *his* son is ashamed of him; Climate is what you expect, Weather is what you get; and income tax lets you work for the government without taking a civil service exam.

Chuckle du jour:

A Caboose is a drunken taxi.

Association News:

The Economic Oversight Task Force wonders if you ever thought you'd see the day when "Dollars to Doughnuts" was an even bet; feels that at least the huge national debt will put an end to ancestor worship; and guesses that behind every successful man is a dedicated woman . . . trying to get his job.

❖

JUST GIVE ME SOME FRESH, NEW IDEAS THAT ARE TRIED AND TRUE

❖

FREE ADVICE IS USUALLY WORTH
ALMOST AS MUCH AS IT COSTS

Chuckle du jour:

Few things are more expensive than a girl who is free for the evening.

Association News:

The Association's Committee on Useful Definitions has decreed that a Bigamist is an Italian fog; a Committee is a device to share the blame with; and a Friend is one who takes you to lunch even when you're not deductible.

Chuckle du jour:

To be loved, get rich and keep revising your will.

Association News:

The Association's Whyizit Committee is exploring: Whyizit that *after* you manage to get the some-assembly-required toy put together, the instructions are so easy to understand? Whyizit some fishermen think big fish should bite on a fancy lure just because they did? And whyizit the easiest way to find something you've lost is to buy a replacement?

❖

BY THE TIME YOU'RE OLD ENOUGH TO BE NOSTALGIC YOUR MEMORY'S TOO SHORT

❖

TASTE MAKES WAIST

Chuckle du jour:

A lawyer is a fellow who can write ten thousand words and call it a brief.

Association News:

The Association's Committee on Old-Fashioned Sexual Relations has determined that a Fox is a Wolf who sends flowers; that the honeymoon is over when your wife complains about the noise you make while fixing breakfast; and that the perfect solution for the man who has everything is the woman who knows exactly what to do with it.

Chuckle du jour:

Almost everything in life is easier to get into than out of.

Association News:

The Association's Committee on Gratuitous Advice wants members to recognize the folly of mixing gunpowder and alcohol: the mix won't fire and it tastes awful; the best cure for insomnia is to try your best to stay awake; and if your teenage son wants to learn to drive, don't stand in his way.

❖

SOME MISTAKES ARE TOO MUCH FUN TO MAKE ONLY ONCE

❖

THE MEEK SHALL INHERIT THE WORK

Chuckle du jour:

Inheritance of the Earth would be OK if the Meek could just be depended upon to stay that way.

Association News:

The Association's Whyizit Committee wants to know: Whyizit people who don't know Right from Wrong always pick wrong? Whyizit doctors won't make house calls but termites will? And whyizit people who can't say anything nice about anybody are so much fun to talk to?

Chuckle du jour:

Teamwork is essential. It lets you blame someone else.

Association News:

The Association's Committee on Logical Conclusions has concluded that most Disasters You Worry About never happen and Disasters That Happen are the ones you haven't worried about; therefore, the more different disasters you worry about, the fewer disasters are left to happen. If you start worrying more about what you haven't been worrying about, you'll keep more disasters from happening. Happiness, consequently, is obtained by worrying about more things.

❖

THERE IS NO SUCH THING AS PETTY CASH

❖

❖

ALWAYS DRIVE COURTEOUSLY—
THE NEXT DRIVER MAY BE IN UNIFORM

❖

Chuckle du jour:

Experience is a great teacher. No man wakes his second baby just to see it smile.

Association News:

The Association's permanent How Come? Committee wants to know: How come those who buy gold mines often get only the shaft? How come being a good liver gives you such a bad liver that you're likely to become a short liver? And how come when some people drink they see double and feel single?

Chuckle du jour:

Nowadays the only way to get a good high school education is to enroll in the college of your choice.

Association News:

The Association's permanent Committee on Deep Thoughts has concluded that: The less you bet, the more you lose when you win; nobody wants to stop living just because of the high cost of it; and you never know how good your memory is until you try to forget something.

❖

KEEP AMERICA BEAUTIFUL
THROW SOMETHING LOVELY AWAY

❖

TIME WOUNDS ALL HEELS

Chuckle du jour:

Why do people who laugh at gypsy fortune-tellers take economists seriously?

Association News:

The Association's Committee on Peculiarities reports this month that: Memory is like a Policeman—never around when you need it; bright eyes indicate curiosity, but black eyes indicate too much; and an Attic is where you store the kind of junk you would throw away if you didn't have an attic.

Chuckle du jour:

For a really quick energy boost, nothing beats having the boss walk in.

Association News:

The Association's ad hoc On-the-Other-Hand Committee reports that: If God had listened to the permissivists, He'd have given Moses Ten Suggestions; a pessimist feels bad when he feels good because he knows he's going to feel worse when he feels bad; and resisting temptation is so difficult because one doesn't want to discourage it completely.

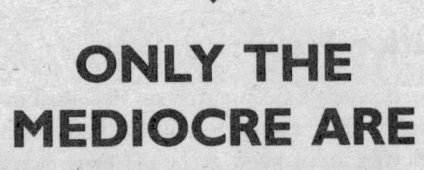

❖

ONLY THE MEDIOCRE ARE
ALWAYS AT THEIR BEST

❖

❖

WORRY KILLS MORE PEOPLE THAN WORK
BECAUSE MORE PEOPLE WORRY THAN WORK

❖

Chuckle du jour:

The easiest way to reduce your bills is to put them on microfilm.

Association News:

The LHBMA,I. Committee on Adaptions and Changes reports that: As people get older, they find work a lot less fun and fun a lot more work; a Luxury becomes a Necessity as soon as you can make a down payment on it; and Experience has a high price but a low resale value.

Chuckle du jour:

Nobody squawks about being interrupted by applause.

Association News:

The Association's standing ad hoc Committee on Whyizit wants to know: Whyizit leftover nuts never match leftover bolts? Whyizit checks are always late in the mail, while bills arrive sooner than expected? And whyizit when you hit two keys on a typewriter, the one you don't want hits the paper?

❖

SELF-PRAISE MAY BE SICKENING
BUT AT LEAST IT'S SINCERE

❖

HIRE TEENAGERS NOW WHILE THEY STILL KNOW EVERYTHING

Chuckle du jour:

It would be a great world if everyone were half as pleasant as the confidence man who's about to skin you.

Association News:

The Association's Committee on Paradox points out that when you take a girl in your arms, you may soon have her on your hands; that if you want someone to feel bad, just give him some good advice; and that bowlers claim the way to get kids off the streets is to send them to the alleys.

Chuckle du jour:

Work is when you'd rather be doing something else.

Association News:

A special LHBMA,I. Committee on Counter Coordinates reports that people who agree with you in principle never mean to carry it out in practice; tact consists of knowing how far is too far; and the guy who tells you what kind of a person he is usually isn't. They applaud the fact that MadaM spelled backward is at least consistent.

❖

DO IT NOW!
TOMORROW THERE'LL BE A LAW AGAINST IT

❖

TO ERR IS HUMAN
TO REALLY FOUL THINGS UP TAKES A COMPUTER

Chuckle du jour:

Politicians try to get money from the rich and votes from the poor by promising to protect each from the other.

Association News:

The Association's Search for Philosophical Answers has learned that old age and treachery will always conquer mere youth and skill; that you can now get dinner at a good hotel for what you used to have to pay for a used car; and that some people get credit for patience when they're just too lazy to argue.

Chuckle du jour:

The less you know about how sausages are made, the better they taste.

Association News:

The Association's Better Definitions Contest, with a ten thousand dollar first prize for best definition, produced only inferior efforts such as: a Shin is a radar device for finding furniture in the dark; a Desk is a wastebasket with drawers; and a Sweater is something a child wears when its mother feels chilly. All three were declared tied for second place.

❖

DON'T THINK OF ME AS SUPERIOR BUT SIMPLY AS A FRIEND WHO ALWAYS JUST HAPPENS TO BE RIGHT

❖

HE WHO LAUGHS LAST
HAD TO HAVE IT EXPLAINED

Chuckle du jour:

Never argue with the fellow who packs your parachute.

Association News:

The Philosophy Committee is now trying to figure out whether you should slow down because you're older than you've ever been or speed up because you're younger than you'll ever be . . . and how people can know so much when you try to tell them something yet so little when you try to ask them something. It is also slightly puzzling the way people seem to refer, fondly, to "the *Good* Old *Days*" when you know that they're really thinking about "the *Bad* Old *Nights*."

Chuckle du jour:

Everything's relative: Break a mirror at ninety-eight and you'll *rejoice* in facing seven years of bad luck.

Association News:

The ad hoc Committee on Aging has determined that forty is a glorious age to be, especially when you're fifty or more; and that Middle Age can be defined as when you'd rather not have a good time than have to get over it and when you can still work as hard as you ever could but simply don't want to.

❖

ABSTINENCE IS GOOD FOR YOU
IF PRACTICED IN MODERATION

❖

OF ALL THE NASTY, LOW-DOWN, FOUL, DIRTY SCHEMES I'VE EVER HEARD, I LIKE YOURS THE BEST

Chuckle du jour:

Many a self-made man quit just a wee bit early.

Association News:

The Association's ad hoc Committee on Incidental Intelligence has determined that most people don't really care if they're rich or not as long as they can live comfortably and have everything they want; that by the time a man can read women like a book, he's too old to go to the library; and the trouble with Experience as a teacher is that the test comes first and the lesson comes afterward.

Chuckle du jour:

If some politicians ran for office unopposed, the election would end in a tie.

Association News:

The Association's Committee on Amazement is amazed that those who can tell the difference between good advice and bad advice bother to ask advice; that fellows who can "marry any girl I please" never seem to please any; and that being rich means you can afford to buy the stuff you don't want anymore.

BEHIND EVERY SUCCESSFUL MAN
IS THE INTERNAL REVENUE SERVICE

MAKE SOMEONE HAPPY TODAY
LOSE YOUR WALLET

Chuckle du jour:

The major side effect of medical treatment today is bankruptcy.

Association News:

The Association's Efficiency Committee suggests: To get something done do it yourself, hire somebody else, or forbid your kids to do it; to get 'em to work on time provide ninety-five parking spaces for every hundred employees; and to lose weight don't talk about it—simply keep your mouth shut.

Chuckle du jour:

Some people are willing to spend an hour sharpening a knife just to whittle a stick.

Association News:

The Association's Committee on the Price of Progress looks back lovingly at the day when a pie was set out to cool rather than to thaw; when solving economic problems brought solutions rather than new problems; and when politicians could only fool *some* of the people all of the time.

❖

MILLIONS ARE IDLE
BUT LUCKILY MOST OF THEM HAVE JOBS

❖

THE TOUGH PART ABOUT MAKING A LIVING IS YOU HAVE TO DO IT ALL OVER AGAIN TOMORROW

Chuckle du jour:

There's nothing like a little experience to upset a perfectly good theory.

Association News:

The Association's GOD (Good Old Daze) Committee notes that you used to be able to rent a car for a week for what it now costs to park it for a day; it used to take two people to carry out fifteen dollars' worth of groceries, but now a child can do it; and that a Genius used to be a Crackpot until the screwball idea worked after all.

Chuckle du jour:

If computers get too powerful, we can organize them into committees—that'll do them in.

Association News:

The Association's Committee on Perception reports that you just can't tell about a dress: Ten years too early, it's "indecent"; a year before its time, it's "daring"; then for one year it's "chic"; but two or three years later "dowdy"; twenty years later it's "hideous"; thirty years later "quaint"; and after a hundred years it's "beautiful." They also define an Optimist as one who reaches for his car keys when the speaker first says, "And, in conclusion. . . ."

❖

HUMILITY IS NOT ONE OF MY FAULTS
BUT IF I HAD ONE, THAT WOULD BE IT

❖

❖

ALL VISITORS BRING HAPPINESS
SOME BY COMING; SOME BY GOING

❖

Chuckle du jour:

Behind every successful man is a woman who couldn't have been more surprised.

Association News:

The Association's standing Committee on Mysterious Compulsions has determined that: Only one person in 2,345 can keep his hands in his pockets when giving directions to a motorist or when describing a circular staircase; travel not only broadens the mind, it also lengthens the conversations; and Misery not only loves Company, it usually insists on it.

Chuckle du jour:

Most people are over-the-hill before they get to the top.

Association News:

The Association's Research Committee reports that: There is something to heredity: the grandparent who thought nothing of walking four miles to school has a grandchild who doesn't think much of it either; ministers are still against sin but can no longer agree on what qualifies; and the average man has sixty-six pounds of muscle and three pounds of brains, which explains just about everything.

❖

DON'T ACCEPT YOUR DOG'S ADMIRATION AS CONCLUSIVE

❖

❖

LIFE IS ONE LONG PROCESS OF GETTING TIRED

❖

Chuckle du jour:

Money can't buy happiness, but it makes misery easier to handle.

Association News:

The Association's Committee on Misplaced Memories reminds you that: Your first big shock came when you realized ice-cream cones weren't filled all the way to the bottom; people used to work eight hours, play eight hours, and sleep eight hours, but not the same eight hours; and an Old-Timer is one old enough to remember when an elderly person was called an Old-Timer.

Chuckle du jour:

A Martyr is a person who is married to a saint.

Association News:

It's the season for a report from the Association's Committee on Political Clarification, which has discovered that: It isn't Freedom *of* Speech that's so important but Freedom *after* Speech; in some circles an honest politician is one who, when bought, stays bought; and a Liberal is a Radical with a wife and child, while a Conservative is a Liberal with property.

❖

WELL-INFORMED CITIZENS ARE THOSE WHO VOTE MY WAY

❖

I THOUGHT I WAS GOING PLACES
BUT I WAS BEING TAKEN

Chuckle du jour:

Experience is a great teacher, but her pupils won't listen.

Association News:

The Association's Do-They-Mean-What-They-Say Committee points out that one and one doesn't always make eleven; that some people who say they have a clean conscience simply mean it's never been used; and crime may not pay, but at least it doesn't claim that the check is in the mail.

Chuckle du jour:

Hospital billing departments should be called "Intensive Scare."

Association News:

The Association's Refocus Committee feels we should quit spending so much time improving hearing aids and work more on what there is to hear . . . and stop worrying about getting old and worry more about not.

❖

MY JOB IS VERY SECURE
IT'S ME THEY CAN DO WITHOUT

❖

POVERTY IS CATCHING
YOU CAN GET IT FROM YOUR RELATIVES

Chuckle du jour:

The nice thing about loafing is that you don't have to exert yourself to show you approve of it.

Association News:

The Association's standing Committee on Unusual Connections reports conclusive findings they believe tend to indicate that borrowing money is excessively injurious to the memory; that while stupidity doesn't kill you, it can frequently make you sweat; and that drinking to your health isn't quite enough to make the dinner a medical deduction.

Chuckle du jour:

Why marry a girl who makes biscuits like Mother if you can find one who makes dough like Father?

Association News:

The Association's Committee on Wandering Words pauses to point out that: Middle Age is when work is no longer play and play is beginning to become work; war is better at abolishing nations than nations are at abolishing war; and Fresh Air is when you open a window, a Draft when someone else does.

❖

THE PENALTY FOR BIGAMY IS TWO MOTHERS-IN-LAW

❖

BEHIND EVERY SUCCESSFUL MAN IS A WOMAN
(TELLING HIM HE IS DOING EVERYTHING WRONG)

Chuckle du jour:

The young and old know all the answers; in between, we can't even be sure of the questions.

Association News:

The Association's Committee on Teenagers has discovered that teens are unhappiest with parents who think they know more than their kids and that their greatest hope is that heredity will be declared unconstitutional. The committee also reports that the major thing wrong with the younger generation is that we don't belong to it.

Chuckle du jour:

Bureaucracy defends the status quo long past the time when the quo has lost its status.

Association News:

Our Remember-Now-That-We're-into-a-New-Year-You're-Going-to-Have-Another-Birthday Committee notes that Middle Age begins when you feel bad in the morning without having had any fun the night before, your back begins to go out more than you do, and you still think you'll be as fit as ever after a good night's sleep.

THE TROUBLE WITH DOING NOTHING IS
THAT YOU CAN'T TELL WHEN TO QUIT

❖

FREE SPEECH IS OFTEN
PRICED EXACTLY RIGHT

❖

Chuckle du jour:

In the old days when a kid misbehaved to get attention, he really got some.

Association News:

The Association's Committee on Better Definitions reports that an Optimist is a man who marries his secretary and thinks he can just go on dictating to her; Memory is what tells you you know the guy, but won't let go of his name; and Diet is a short period of starvation followed by an immediate gain of five pounds.

Chuckle du jour:

Nothing makes a good listener as much as thin motel walls.

Association News:

Our Double-Decade Task Force has found that we change every twenty years: At twenty we worry about what others think about us; at forty we don't care what they think about us; at sixty we discover they haven't been thinking about us at all. Two other aging milestones they discovered are: when you sit in a rocking chair but can't get it going, and when you finally know all the answers but they quit asking you questions.

❖

IN ORDER TO SAVE FACE KEEP THE BOTTOM HALF SHUT

❖

WE LIVE BY THE GOLDEN RULE
THE GUY WITH THE GOLD MAKES THE RULE

Chuckle du jour:

A recent survey shows the prettiest college girls like older men—but they think "older" is about thirty-three.

Association News:

The Association's Economics Committee has declared: Money is a highly overrated commodity: you can't buy happiness with it, or love, or peace of mind. It will not heal the cut of an angry word, nor rejoin the pieces of a shattered dream. It is a sham, a fraud, as false a friend as man has ever seen. Further investigation indicates they were speaking of confederate money.

Chuckle du jour:

Never forget: *You* are one of those who can be fooled some of the time.

Association News:

The Association's Committee on Cause and Effect is investigating how such hopeless sons-in-law can become the fathers of such brilliant grandchildren; their Cause-of-Sickness Subcommittee is stumped by the way kids who gag on spinach grow up to love yogurt; and their chairman wonders why things never seem to be lost except when you're looking where they aren't.

❖

LET'S ALL WORK TOGETHER AS A TEAM
EVERYBODY DO AS I SAY

❖

❖

DON'T CRITICIZE YOUR WIFE:
IF SHE WERE PERFECT,
SHE'D HAVE MARRIED BETTER

❖

Chuckle du jour:

Whatever it is that makes some people tick sure needs winding.

Association News:

The Association's Historical Committee reports that Hard Times are when we have to do without what our grandparents never even imagined was possible; that living in the past may seem foolish to some, but the price sure is right; and that no one ever really gets old-enough-to-know-better.

Chuckle du jour:

The great value of a polka-dot tie is that one more spot won't hurt.

Association News:

Our standing Committee on Life-styles has determined that the very best way to get real enjoyment out of a garden is to put on a floppy straw hat, dress in old clothes that you don't mind soiling, hold a trowel in one hand and a cool drink in the other—and tell the gardener where to dig. They also maintain that the only ones who ever brag about childhood poverty are the safely rich, and that some folks have now become so scared reading about the dangers of smoking that they've finally decided, cold turkey, to stop reading.

❖

THE SQUEAKING WHEEL ALSO GETS REPLACED

❖

❖

IF GOD HAD MEANT US TO TRAVEL TOURIST HE WOULD HAVE MADE US NARROWER

❖

Chuckle du jour:

Punctuality is a scheme for getting some time for yourself.

Association News:

The Association's Committee on Unexpected Solutions has concluded that any husband can help his wife make up her mind just by voicing his own opinion; lost objects are always found in the very last place you expect to find them; and the cheapest way to have your family tree traced is to run for public office.

Chuckle du jour:

You'll never make ends meet if you're always sitting on yours.

Association News:

In the interest of testing the accuracy of old myths and superstitions, the Association's Computer Committee has determined that the chances of bread falling butter-side down are directly proportional to the cost of the carpet beneath; that rich, childless relatives live 33.5 percent longer than poor ones; and that narrow, closed minds are 100 percent likely to have wide, open mouths.

❖

LEND MONEY TO FRIENDS
IT RUINS THEIR MEMORY

❖

❖

A WOMAN'S PLACE IS IN THE HOME
AS SOON AS SHE CAN GET THERE AFTER WORK

❖

Chuckle du jour:

Teenagers get homesick only when they're home.

Association News:

The LHBMA, I.'s Directors Committee has determined that: Duels never prove who is right, only who is left; the best way to help your kids with their arithmetic is not to; and when your outgo exceeds your income, your upkeep becomes your downfall.

Chuckle du jour:

How come faith healers don't do teeth?

Association News:

The Association's Committee on Clarifying Definitions has determined that: Heredity is what sets the parents of teenagers wondering about each other; an Optimist is one who considers marriage a gamble; and Compromise is what you will agree to today that you swore last week you would never be found dead doing.

❖

HELP PEOPLE IN TROUBLE AND THEY'LL ALWAYS REMEMBER YOU
WHENEVER THEY'RE IN TROUBLE AGAIN

❖

MONEY CAN BE LOST IN MORE WAYS THAN WON

Chuckle du jour:

A budget helps you pay as you go by not letting you go anywhere.

Association News:

The Association's Committee on Money reports that if you want to become rich, just find something to sell that's low-priced, habit-forming, nonfattening, and tax-deductible. They also found that the only way to keep food bills down this year is to use *very* heavy paperweights, and that nowadays the best thing that can happen when you go shopping for bargains is to not be able to find what you want.

Chuckle du jour:

Nowadays a rare steak is one that's the same price as last week.

Association News:

The Association's Finance Committee reports that: Research shows the most expensive per-mile vehicle to operate is a supermarket cart; money in the bank is like toothpaste in a tube—easy to get out, hard to get back in; and the best way to get your car to run better is to ask the price of a new one.

❖

A FOOL AND HIS MONEY ARE SOON INVITED PLACES

❖

IF AT FIRST YOU DON'T SUCCEED CHECK THE TRASH FOR THE INSTRUCTIONS

Chuckle du jour:

Wall-to-wall carpeting is hard to beat.

Association News:

The Association's Study of the Divergence of Thought and Action has concluded that: The best way to get a good night's sleep is to have a bad one the night before; the only thing worse than a flooded basement is a flooded attic; and the only surefire way to develop good judgment is bad judgment.

Chuckle du jour:

The leading cause of death among laboratory mice is research.

Association News:

The Association's Committee on Rational Reasoning wants to know: How come Chinese fortune cookies are always written in English? What in the world happens to sour cream when it spoils? And whyizit that Abbreviation is such a long word?

❖

NEPOTISM'S NOT SO BAD
IF YOU KEEP IT IN THE FAMILY

❖

BY THE TIME THE KIDS ARE FIT TO LIVE WITH THEY'RE LIVING WITH SOMEONE ELSE

Chuckle du jour:

Lots of people now wish they were what they were when they wished they were what they are now.

Association News:

The Association's Committee on the Next Generation reports that: The problem with kids' questions begins when the questions start having answers; teenagers were invented to keep parents from wasting time on the phone; and kids love criticism as long as it's unqualified praise.

Chuckle du jour:

A man may have more money than brains, but not for long.

Association News:

The Association's Committee on Today's Problems reports that a country has to be in trouble when it takes more brains to make out an income tax form than it takes to make the income; that if pollution doesn't stop soon, the muck will inherit the earth; and that it's easier to vote a straight party ticket than it is to find a straight party.

❖

A PENNY SAVED IS A PENNY TAXED

❖

❖

LONG WALKS ARE HEALTHY
WHY DON'T YOU TAKE ONE?

❖

Chuckle du jour:

Summer is better than winter because you don't have to shovel sunshine.

Association News:

Our research group Searching for the *Real* Reason has determined that mountain climbers really rope themselves together to keep the sensible ones from going home; that bald men like it that way because when company comes, all they have to do is straighten their ties; and that most people who get credit for patience simply can't get up the nerve to start anything.

Chuckle du jour:

Nothing puts weight on a fish like a lone fisherman.

Association News:

The Association's People Committee, searching for Eternal Truths, has determined that anyone who says he enjoys a cold shower in the morning will lie about other things, too; that a true friend is one who takes a winter vacation on a sun-drenched beach and doesn't send you a picture postcard; and that people who hire people who are smarter than they are, are smarter than the people they hire.

❖

I'VE MADE ONLY ONE MISTAKE THIS YEAR I THOUGHT I WAS WRONG; TURNED OUT TO BE RIGHT

❖

NEVER UNDERESTIMATE A WOMAN UNLESS YOU'RE ESTIMATING AGE OR WEIGHT

Chuckle du jour:

Confidence is that positive feeling you have before you discover you're wrong.

Association News:

The Association's Committee on Definitions indicates that Maintenance-Free really means that when it breaks it can't be fixed; Antiques are what you forgot to throw away before they got valuable; and a Bargain is something you can't use at a price you can't resist.

Chuckle du jour:

You're a success when your income tax equals what you used to dream of earning.

Association News:

The Association's chief researcher this month focused on the initial unproductiveness of effort, trying to discover why celebrities work so hard to become famous, then wear dark glasses so they won't be recognized; why so many women who buy Crockpots to cook slow and microwave ovens to cook fast never learn how to cook right; and why by the time you really have experience, you're too old to get a job.

❖

A MAN WHO CAN SMILE WHEN THINGS GO WRONG
HAS FOUND SOMEONE HE CAN BLAME IT ON

❖

❖

SAVE STRING
WHILE YOU'RE YOUNG
LATER ON YOU'LL HAVE A BALL

❖

Chuckle du jour:

The only place to get more for your money today is on a penny scale.

Association News:

The Association's investigators of Space-Age Life have determined that an attic is better than a garage because you don't have to keep cleaning it out to make way for the car; that the older a man gets, the farther he had to walk to school as a boy; and that faith may move mountains, but it sure meets its match with surplus fat.

Chuckle du jour:

Anyone can give advice; the trick is to find a taker.

Association News:

The Association's ad hoc Font-of-Wisdom Committee reports, or advises, as the case may be: Of two evils, choose the prettier; opening days of school are the most wonderful days of your life, provided your kids are old enough to go; in life, some object to the fan dancer, others object to the fan; and RadaR is RadaR spelled backward.

❖

ALCOHOL PRESERVES EVERYTHING EXCEPT SECRETS

❖

EVERYONE HAS SOME VALUE IF ONLY AS A HORRIBLE EXAMPLE

Chuckle du jour:

Forecasting is only difficult when you do it about the future.

Association News:

In his never-ending taste for truth, the Association's night watchman has discovered that martini drinkers get more tooth cavities than milk drinkers but visit dentists in a happier frame of mind; that anyone can cure insomnia just by pretending it's time to get up and go to work; and that the basic reason for marriage is that sometimes things go wrong that you just can't blame on the government.

Chuckle du jour:

One of the great pleasures of giving a party is having it over.

Association News:

Members recently visited Las Vegas and found it is possible to quit while ahead; while it's true that all odds are with the house, there's always a chance someone will drop a wallet, which you can kick away and examine at leisure. Their next assignment will be to find out why school-bus drivers always break down before school buses. After that they'll examine IRS agents, carefully avoiding the vice versa, and then determine why anyone would bother to invent a better mousetrap to get the world to beat a path to his door when he can do it just by taking an afternoon nap.

❖

POLITICAL BEDFELLOWS SHARE THE SAME BUNK

❖

❖

RESIST YE NOT FROM TEMPTATION
IT MAY NOT PASS THIS WAY AGAIN

❖

Chuckle du jour:

One good thing about humidity—stamps stick to envelopes.

Association News:

The Association has appointed a standing committee to investigate the perversity of the human condition: Why, for instance, does the radio always tell us the temperature at the airport when it's the temperature at the bus stop that counts? How come the best way to get undivided attention is to tell someone it's none of their business? And why do too many square meals make round people?

Chuckle du jour:

A couple with six children is more satisfied than a couple with six million dollars—when you have six million dollars, you still want more.

Association News:

The Association's Q&A Committee wants to know: Whyizit the first half of a task takes 90 percent of the allotted time and the second half takes the other 90 percent? Whyizit as soon as parents teach kids to walk and talk they tell them to sit down and shut up? And how come Economy Size means big in soap and small in automobiles?

❖

IF AT FIRST YOU DON'T SUCCEED
TRY PLAYING SECOND

❖

IF AT FIRST YOU DON'T SUCCEED,
FIX THE BLAME QUICK

Chuckle du jour:

A cocktail party is a place where drinks mix people.

Association News:

The Association's ad hoc Committee organized a Food Focus Group to study dieting and why so much food nowadays goes to waist. He's found only one woman who weighs the same as in high school—she was forty pounds overweight then. . . . But they recommend the surefire Chinese diet: all the rice you can eat but only one chopstick. Next month they will try to figure out why so many people hate any kind of change that doesn't jingle in their pockets.

Chuckle du jour:

For really successful farming: Rise early, work hard, and arrange to strike oil with your plow.

Association News:

Our treasurer has recently measured the ratio of horse sense to nonsense in normal conversation, discovering that those who talk the most say the least and that the only improvement possible is for those who usually have nothing to say to say nothing more often. In much the same vein he's found that girls who know the least about what to cook know the most about what's cookin . . . and the Horn of Plenty is the one in the car behind you the instant the light turns green.

❖

THE BEST FLINGS IN LIFE AIN'T FREE

❖

❖

MONEY ISN'T EVERYTHING AS LONG AS YOU HAVE PLENTY

❖

Chuckle du jour:

If it jams, force it; if it breaks, it was no good anyway.

Association News:

The LHBMA, I. research team has focused on minor mysteries of life recently, primarily searching for penetrating questions rather than spending time on answers, which usually turn out to be wrong anyway. What is it about wearing a tuxedo, they want to know, that always gives you a headache the next morning? How come long skirts make girls look shorter while short skirts make boys look longer? And whyizit American tourists will go anywhere except to the rear of the bus?

Chuckle du jour:

If meeting new people is a problem for you, try picking up the wrong ball on the golf course.

Association News:

The Association's Committee on Daffynitions proposes that an Igloo is the sticky stuff that keeps an Ig from coming apart; that Conscience is what feels so bad when everything else feels so good; and that a Scandinavian Myth is a Laplander lath who kithith under the mithletoe.

❖

HARD WORK NEVER KILLED ANYONE
BUT WHY RISK BEING THE FIRST?

❖

MAYBE MONEY WON'T GO AS FAR TODAY BUT IT SURE GOES FASTER

Chuckle du jour:

Remember: THE IRS spells THEIRS.

Association News:

The Association's Committee on Money and Credit tells us that a dime is as valuable as it ever was—when used as a screwdriver; that inflation lets us live in more expensive neighborhoods without even moving; and that it takes losers to make winners possible, so pitch in.

Chuckle du jour:

By the time a man gets to greener pastures he can't climb the fence.

Association News:

The Association is considering the production of a handbook for honest politicians, a market that may not exhaust the first printing. It will point out that success in politics doesn't take know-how, it takes know-who; that perhaps the only nice thing about being in politics is that your wife doesn't knock you in public; and warn that contrary to common sense, skating on thin ice is likely to get you in hot water.

❖

SUPPORT AGRICULTURE— SOW MORE WILD OATS

❖

❖

PEOPLE WHO LIVE IN GLASS HOUSES SHOULDN'T GET STONED

❖

Chuckle du jour:

In a small town, it's no sooner done than said.

Association News:

The Association's Task Force on Aging Youthfully tells us it's no use wishing to be young again—just concentrate on getting older; that people who insist on living in the past know one thing about it—it's cheaper; and that old age brings us wisdom, and wisdom tells us, among other things, that they don't make mirrors like they used to.

Chuckle du jour:

Artificial mistletoe works just as well as the real thing.

Association News:

The Association's Committee on Progress tells us that Television was better when it was Radio; Computers get more work done than people because they don't have to answer the phone; and you have to avoid temptation when you're young because later on it avoids you.

❖

THE CUSTOMER IS ALWAYS RIGHT!
MISINFORMED, INEXACT, BULLHEADED, FICKLE, STUPID, AND FORGETFUL MAYBE, BUT NEVER WRONG

❖

❖

FIRING WILL CONTINUE AROUND HERE UNTIL MORALE IMPROVES

❖

Chuckle du jour:

Nothing seems to make a person quite so stupid as driving the car ahead of you.

Association News:

The Association's Committee on Food and Associated Vices points out that the nice thing about ordering beer is that nobody asks you what year you want; philosophers lie awake trying to decide what happens to the hole when the cheese is gone; and Drugs are substances that, when fed to mice, produce horrifying scientific reports.

Chuckle du jour:

The first thing a kid learns when he gets a drum for Christmas is that he won't get another one.

Association News:

The Association's Fitness Committee tells us that Middle Age is when anything different in the way you feel is a symptom; that Kleptomania is one of the easiest of all diseases to treat—you can take almost anything for it; and that Car Sickness is the feeling you get every month when the payment's due.

❖

ANYTHING WORTH DOING IS WORTH HIRING SOMEONE WHO KNOWS HOW TO DO IT

❖

PEOPLE WHO THINK THEY KNOW IT ALL REALLY ANNOY THOSE OF US WHO DO

Chuckle du jour:

Inflation is when you need a double-your-money-back guarantee just to break even.

Association News:

The Association's Geriatrics Committee has put out an all-points bulletin for members who can remember when penny candy was only a nickel, rather than fifteen cents . . . or recall when they could pick up a handkerchief with their teeth instead of vice versa . . . or even when it took more time to fly across the country than it took to get to the airport.

Chuckle du jour:

There are more important things in life than money, but none of them will go out with you when you're broke.

Association News:

The Association's Meditation and Philosophy Committee addresses with emphasis the more basic questions of life, such as "Is Nothing part of Everything?"; and "If you can't get Something for Nothing, what does the other fellow get when you get Nothing for Something, which happens all the time?"; and "If the meek do inherit the earth, who'll collect overdue bills?"

❖

JUST BECAUSE YOU HAVE A JOB
DON'T FEEL YOU MUST STOP LOOKING FOR WORK

❖

IF YOU THINK THE PROBLEM'S BAD NOW JUST WAIT UNTIL CONGRESS SOLVES IT

Chuckle du jour:

Any job that isn't work is already filled by a relative.

Association News:

After three weeks of trying to find out what goes into chicken soup, the Association's Executive Committee has decided to give up kitchen-type cooking and return to philosophy, where they are more at home cooking up questions like: If medical men advertise, will surgeons offer cut rates? How come women get such a big charge out of credit cards? How old are you when, by the time you find your glasses, you can't remember why you wanted them? And why do nonsmokers fume so much?

Chuckle du jour:

Politicians used to be able to buy a whole ward for approximately what one minute of TV costs now.

Association News:

The Association has declared this to be *Why* month and has offered as starters: Why do we put leftovers in the refrigerator for a week before throwing them out? Why are the shoes that fit always the wrong color? And why, when gals finally get themselves starved down to a decent weight, do fellows finally start inviting them out to dinner?

❖

I NEVER GET ANGRY
I GET EVEN

❖

I DON'T WANT TO START ANY ARGUMENT
I JUST WANT TO EXPLAIN WHY YOU'RE WRONG

Chuckle du jour:

A supermarket is where you spend thirty minutes looking for instant coffee.

Association News:

Our medical group reports a general yearning for the good old romantic days . . . when air pollution was called stardust and there was still such a thing as a small taxpayer. They predict that most of today's ills would quickly disappear if everyone was completely sincere, whether they meant it or not. They're also for more waste in some government departments . . . if Internal Revenue operations get any more efficient, they'll have to put in a recovery room.

Chuckle du jour:

Some people don't say much; they just won't stop talking.

Association News:

Our new research team has spent the last two weeks studying the ground rules of Perversity. Among other subjects, they've investigated why folk singers get rich by singing about how great it is to be poor; why you used to dream about making the same salary that's now keeping you up nights trying to balance the budget; and why people who tell you how young you look don't realize they're also telling you how old you are.

❖

HELP PRESERVE WILDLIFE
THROW A PARTY TONIGHT

❖

NO AMOUNT OF PLANNING WILL EVER REPLACE DUMB LUCK

Chuckle du jour:

At the current price of apples it's cheaper to use a doctor.

Association News:

An advanced psychology class is hard at work trying to determine why people blame fate for other accidents but feel personally responsible for a hole in one; why folks who say that they never give secrets away are always ready to trade them; and why most trouble starts out being fun.

Chuckle du jour:

Home cooking is where a lot of women aren't.

Association News:

The Association's Committee on Daily Difficulties tells us that the trouble with being an optimist is there is no way you can be pleasantly surprised; the only thing harder than a diamond is making the payments on one; and that making money is easy enough—it's earning a living that's tough.

❖

NEVER MAKE THE SAME MISTAKE TWICE
PLENTY OF NEW ONES ARE AVAILABLE

❖

YOU CAN LEAD A MAN TO CONGRESS BUT YOU CAN'T MAKE HIM THINK

Chuckle du jour:

The only thing more obtuse than a politician's statement is his clarification of it.

Association News:

The Association's inquiring reporter has been trying to determine why people insist that butcher scales be strictly honest but are perfectly willing to have those in the bathroom fudge a bit. He's also curious to learn why they're called appetizers when all they do is spoil your appetite. Next month he expects to spend most of his time lobbying Congress to make all paychecks plus tax and all purchases minus tax instead of vice versa.

Chuckle du jour:

One thing about inviting trouble—it's sure to accept.

Association News:

The Association's Committee on Diminishment has concluded that Advice is what you are going to get when you aren't going to get what you were after; if you don't care where you are, you can never get lost; and most people don't have to turn out the lights to be in the dark.

❖

NOTHING IMPROVES MY HEARING FASTER THAN PRAISE

❖

I AM A POSITIVE THINKER
I'M POSITIVE THAT WON'T WORK

Chuckle du jour:

Financial success will help you find some mighty interesting relatives.

Association News:

The Association's Committee on Words is trying to determine exactly how much cold cash it takes to get people to warm up to you; why there's such a big difference between those who are chaste and those who are chased, and why a shortcut is the longest distance between two points.

Chuckle du jour:

Old Bureaucrats never die—they just waste away.

Association News:

The Association's Economics Committee reports that since yesterday's nest egg won't even serve as today's chicken feed, the question is not whether you can take it with you but whether you'll have enough to get there. They have suggested to the Energy Committee that the first of our country's natural resources to be depleted will probably be the average taxpayer. They also want to know why arguments always have at least two sides but no end.

❖

THANKS FOR OFFERING TO HELP
BUT I DON'T HAVE THE TIME

❖

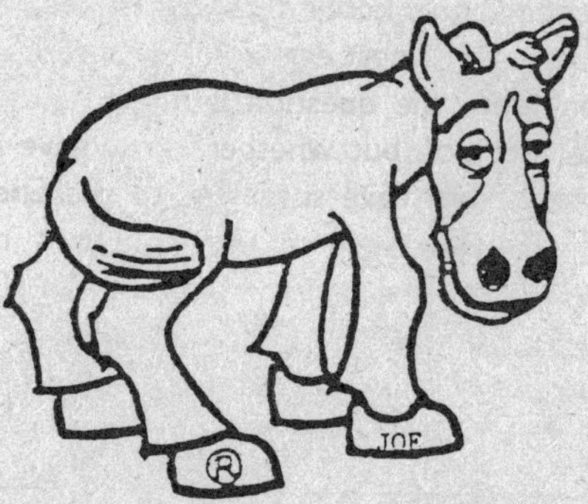
JOE

CHARLIE BROWN, SNOOPY
and the whole **PEANUTS® gang...**

together again with another set of
daily trials and tribulations by

CHARLES M. SCHULZ

Copr. © 1952
United Feature Syndicate, Inc.

Available at your bookstore or use this coupon.

___ GO FOR IT, CHARLIE BROWN   20793 2.95
Vol III, selected from DR. BEAGLE AND MR. HYDE)

___ IT'S CHOW TIME SNOOPY   21355 2.95
(Vol I, selected from DR. BEAGLE AND MR. HYDE)

___ LOOK OUT BEHIND YOU, SNOOPY   21196 2.95
(Vol I from HERE COMES THE APRIL FOOL)

___ GET PHYSICAL, SNOOPY!   20789 3.50

___ LET'S PARTY, CHARLIE BROWN   20600 2.95

FAWCETT MAIL SALES
400 Hahn Road, Westminster, MD 21157

Please send me the FAWCETT BOOKS I have checked above. I am enclosing $ . . . . (add $2.00 to cover postage and handling for the first book and 50¢ each additional book. Please include appropriate state sales tax.) Send check or money order—no cash or C.O.D.'s please. To order by phone, call 1-800-733-3000. Prices are subject to change without notice. Valid in U.S. only. All orders are subject to availability of books.

Name_____

Address_____

City_____ State_____ Zip Code_____

30   Allow at least 4 weeks for delivery   4/92 TAF-3

Information At Your Fingertips

✻

Reference Books from Fawcett

Available at your bookstore or use this coupon.

___ **DICTIONARY OF 20th CENTURY ALLUSIONS**
by Sylvia Cole and A. Lass
449-14743-6 $4.95

___ **DICTIONARY OF CLASSICAL, BIBLICAL, & LITERARY ALLUSIONS**
by Lass, Kiremidjian, and Goldst
449-14565-4 $4.95

___ **SHAKESPEARIAN TRAGEDY**
by A.C. Bradley
449-30035-8 $4.95

FAWCETT MAIL SALES
400 Hahn Road, Westminster, MD 21157

Please send me the FAWCETT BOOKS I have checked above. I am enclosing $ . . . . (add $2.00 to cover postage and handling for the first book and 50¢ each additional book. Please include appropriate state sales tax.) Send check or money order—no cash or C.O.D.'s please. To order by phone, call 1-800-733-3000. Prices are subject to change without notice. Valid in U.S. only. All orders are subject to availability of books.

Name_____

Address_____

City_____ State_____ Zip_____

03   Allow at least 4 weeks for delivery.   7/91   TAF-284